Gokul Village and The Magic Fountain

Written by
Jeni Chapman & Bal Das

Illustrated by
Charlene Chua

High in the faraway hills,
where the air was fresh,
and the sky was deep blue,
lived a very special fountain.

In good times and in bad,
the fountain gave the people of Gokul village
water to drink, wash clothes,
and to splash friends.

But now, people no longer needed the fountain
like they once did. And the fountain sat ignored.

Its orbs were dirty. Its pipes were clogged.
Its water barely flowed anymore.
The fountain was lonely,
except when six friends visited it.

Every morning, these six friends met at the fountain on the way to school. And every afternoon they played there.

Zoya loved to paint and imagine how beautiful the fountain could be.

Christopher was a builder.
He wanted to fix the fountain one day.

Riya played her flute to accompany the sound of the dripping water.

Dalai loved to ride his bicycle. Around and around the fountain he'd go!

Noelle was curious.
She designed iDEA, a drone,
to see the village from high above.

Jacob loved to bake
treats for his friends.

The kids loved the old fountain. After school they pretended the fountain connected to all the rivers and oceans in the world. They imagined going on adventures to other lands.
They sang a special song:

"Waters of the world, connect us this day.

Waters of the world, take us away."

But today they thought of the New Year's party that was only a few days away. Every year, the children decorated the town's square for the big event.

Dalai sped in on his bike to meet his friends. "I have bad news," Dalai announced. "The mayor canceled the celebration. She says the fountain needs repairs and can't be fixed before the party."

"Oh no," Zoya exclaimed. "Our old fountain is beautiful. We have to fix it!"

"I know we can do it if we work together," said Christopher.

Riya jumped to action and said, "Yes, let's do this! I have a plan."

She gave everyone a job.

1. Noelle: Research fountain.
2. Jacob: Make snacks.
3. Zoya/Riya: Replace orbs.
4. Christopher: Fix pipes.
5. Dalai: Repair broken part.

A few hours later, the friends had found what they needed to get the job done. Now they had to convince the mayor they could do it. But how?

Dalai volunteered to help. He said to his friends, "I love talking to people. I will do it."

So Dalai spoke with the mayor. He told her about everything they had already done.

It worked. She offered the kids a compromise. If they could clean up the fountain the celebration wouldn't be canceled.

Hurray!

It was time for **action!**

In two days, the children's teamwork paid off!
No longer were the fountain orbs broken and dusty.
No longer were its pipes clogged.
Now the water flowed freely.
It sparkled!

The mayor arrived to see what the kids had done. She was amazed by the beauty they had created. Right away she said, "The festival is back on."

"We did it team!" cheered Zoya. "I knew we could if we worked together."

The fountain looked happy.

Then, something amazing happened. The fountain glowed with extra shimmer. The water sparkled with extra shine. The orbs radiated extra light. The fountain was granting each of them an extraordinary gift!

Notes from Riya's flute transformed into singing birds.

Zoya's paintbrush splashed beautiful scenes in the air.

The beads of Dalai's bracelet **glowed** with light, like the orbs on the fountain.

Out from Jacob's pack tumbled anything he could imagine for cooking his special dishes.

Christopher's tools grew larger until they tickled the sky.

iDEA, Noelle's drone, flickered to life and started speaking!

"Look in the fountain's heart," iDEA instructed. "There are words hidden there. The fountain wants to thank you."

"Are you actually talking, iDEA?" Noelle gasped.

Dalai spotted the text. He touched the inscription with his fingers and read the words out loud.

THE WORLD IS BIG. ARE YOU BOLD?

WITH MY HELP YOU'LL SOON KNOW.

SAY THE WORDS. WATCH ME GLOW

1, 2, 3...AND OFF YOU GO!

The fountain's orbs got brighter and brighter.
One by one the kids each touched a colored orb.
Together they sang their favorite song:

"Waters of the world, connect us this day.

Waters of the world, take us away."

The fountain's water wrapped itself around them, and they were transported far away.

The kids saw the jostling, jolly New York City crowd celebrating the arrival of the New Year.

And look, there was the Chinese celebration!
They watched millions of people clap and
sway together, hoping for happiness
and good fortune for all.

Then they saw the dazzling glow of the Diwali festival in India, signifying the power of light over darkness.

Then, just as miraculously, they were back.

"Wow! What just happened?" asked Noelle.

"That was the best water ride I have ever been on!" joked Jacob.

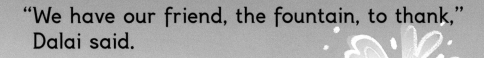

"We have our friend, the fountain, to thank," Dalai said.

Christopher had an idea. "Let's name the fountain Friendship Fountain!" Everyone agreed.

"We have our own celebration to prepare," Zoya reminded them. "Let's make it the best New Year's celebration Gokul has ever seen."

Inspired by their awesome adventure, the kids decorated the town square with treasures from the celebrations they had visited.

The next day, everyone in the village agreed it was the best party ever.

"Do you think we'll share more adventures?" wondered Jacob.

"Let's find out," Zoya laughed. "Dalai, you activated the fountain last time. Try again."

Dalai thought for a moment then whispered, "Friendship Fountain awake, Friendship Fountain activate." Once again his bracelet lit up.

Everyone touched a colored orb,
and they shouted their song together.

"Waters of the world, connect us this day.

Waters of the world, take us away."

And just like that, they were off again.

Where in the world would they go this time?

"To our mothers, who always believed in our own beautiful glows."

CPSIA information can be obtained
at www.ICGtesting.com
Printed in the USA
LVHW07n1759130318
569700LV00015B/331/P